To Scott, Jacqui, Lucas, Kate and Jamie

Love you to the moon and back.

Baby and me.

Written by Sarah McPherson
Illustrated by Lena Serikova

First Printing, 2022

Published by Tarva Publishing
www.tarvapublishing.com.au
www.sarahmcphersonauthor.com.au

ISBN - 978-0-6456769-4-5

Baby and Me

By Sarah McPherson

Illustrated by Lena Serikova

There's a tiny little baby,
growing in my mum.
I cannot wait to meet them,
and see who they become.

Are they a brother or a sister,
I really do not mind.
As long as they can share,
and are very kind.

My babies very special,
they are meant to be.
But its going to be different,
when its not just me.

Mum says that babies kicking,
she says that it's ok.
Mum says that babies happy,
and having a little play.

Now mummy's getting tired,
Her tummy's like a balloon.
Everybody's saying,
the baby's coming soon.

My bed's in babies room now,
I guess I have to share.
I have a special bed now,
I guess that makes it fair.

It's time to meet my baby,
I cannot wait to see.
Do they look like mummy,
Or do they look like me.

My babies very tiny,
little fingers, little toes.
I think they have my ears,
They also have my nose.

So many people visit,
they bring special gifts you see.
Blankets, teddies, and clothing,
and then something nice for me.

I love my little baby,
we are going to have such fun.
My baby and me,
our adventures just begun.

Made in the USA
Middletown, DE
14 January 2023

22164827R00015